For my mum
~ D B
For Andy, Caroline,
Charlotte and Harry
~ T W

LITTLE TIGER PRESS LTD,
an imprint of the Little Tiger Group
1 Coda Studios, 189 Munster Road, London SW6 6AW
www.littletiger.co.uk

First published in Great Britain 2005
This edition published 2014

A CIP catalogue record for this book is available
from the British Library

LTP/1800/2839/0719
Printed in China

4 6 8 10 9 7 5

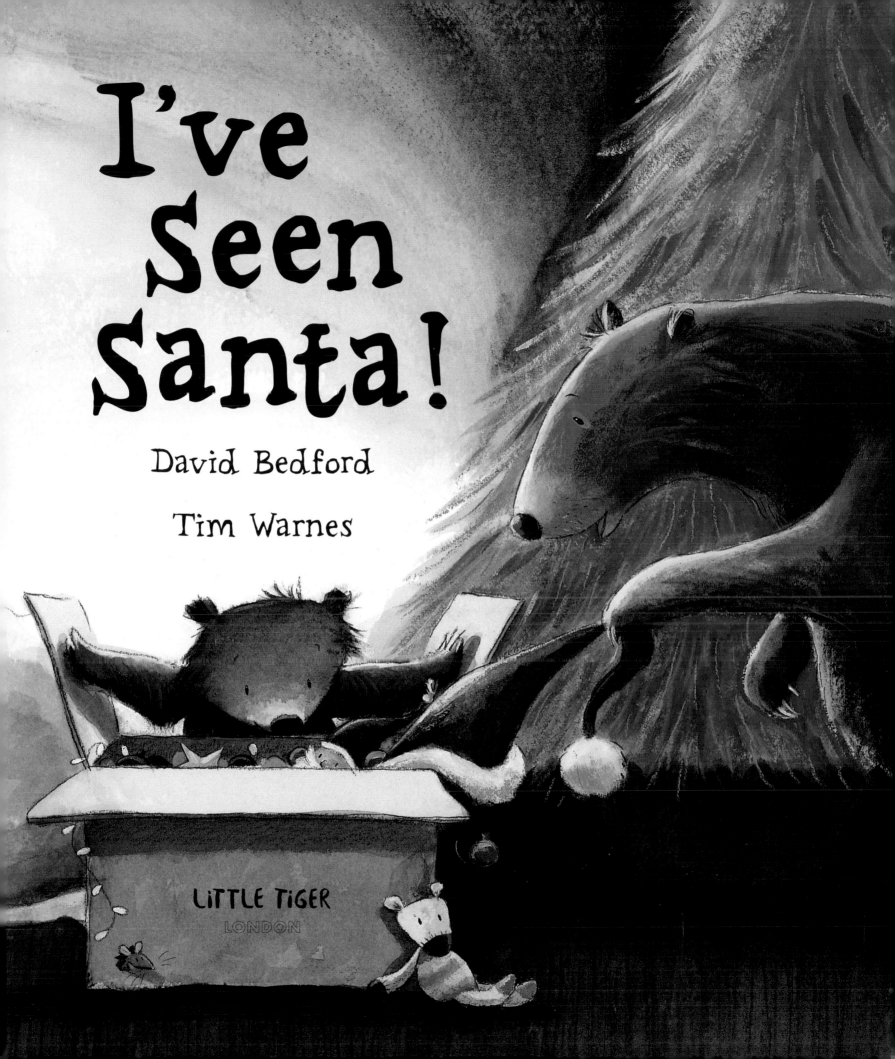

I've Seen Santa!

David Bedford

Tim Warnes

LITTLE TIGER
LONDON

It was Christmas Eve and Little Bear was looking forward to seeing Santa.

"Is Santa as big as you?" he asked Big Bear.

"Nearly," said Big Bear, proudly.

"Oh," said Little Bear, looking worried.
"Will Santa fit down our chimney, then?"
    "Of course he will!" said Big Bear. "I'll show you."
    Big Bear went outside and climbed into
the chimney . . .

CRASH!

"See?" said Big Bear, from a cloud of soot.
"Santa will get in, no problem!"

"Santa won't come if he sees this mess!"
said Mummy Bear.

"We'll help clean up," said Little Bear.

"Does Santa visit bears
all over the world?"
said Little Bear.
"Yes," said Big Bear.
"He goes to every
house."

"Hmm," said Little Bear. "He might not have time to come here, and then I won't have any presents."

"Don't worry," said Mummy Bear. "Santa will come just as soon as you go to sleep."

For SANTA
(paws off
Big Bear)

Little Bear didn't want to go to sleep.
He wanted to see Santa. He listened to
Mummy Bear and Big Bear going to bed.
And then . . . GLUG, GLUG, GLUG, GLUG!

What was that noise?
Someone was downstairs!

Someone big was sitting
by the fireplace.
"Yes!" whispered Little Bear.
"It's Santa! I've seen Santa!"
Little Bear tiptoed up and saw . . .

. . . Big Bear!

"That's Santa's milk!" said Little Bear.
"I only wanted a sip," said Big Bear,
"before I go to sleep." He took Little
Bear's hand. "Come on, Little Bear.
Let's go to bed."

Little Bear tried to stay awake, but he soon fell into a doze.

Then a loud noise downstairs woke him up.

MUNCH! MUNCH! MUNCH! MUNCH!

Someone big was standing
by the Christmas tree.
This time it had to be . . .

. . . Big Bear again!

"You're eating Santa's mince pies now!" said Little Bear.

"I was hungry," said Big Bear.

"If Santa's as greedy as you," said Mummy Bear, coming downstairs, "he'll be too big and he WILL get stuck in the chimney! Now go to bed and go to sleep – both of you!"

Little Bear went to bed, but he couldn't go to sleep. He was too worried. He woke up Big Bear to ask him a question.
   "What if Santa eats too many mince pies and then gets stuck in the chimney?" he whispered.

"Hmm," said Big Bear.

"Let's keep watch to make sure he's OK," said Little Bear. "We can hide so he won't see us."

"Shhh!" whispered Little Bear
from their hiding place.
"I can hear something!
It MUST be Santa this time!"

Someone was putting
presents in their stockings!
Big Bear turned on his
torch to see . . .

. . . Mummy Bear!

"What are YOU doing?" said Big Bear.
"I'm giving you both a present from me,"
said Mummy Bear. "Just in case Santa
is a tiny bit late. What are YOU doing?"
"We're not going to bed," said Big Bear.
"We're going to see Santa!"
squealed Little Bear.

Mummy Bear laughed.
"Make room for me,
then," she said. "We'll
ALL see Santa."

Little Bear, Big Bear and
Mummy Bear stayed downstairs
all through the night.

But they never did see Santa . . .

. . . even though
Santa saw them!

This Little Tiger book belongs to:

_____

_____

_____